THE NO-GOOD DO-GOOD PIRATES

Jim Kraft   illustrated by Lynne Avril

Albert Whitman & Company, Morton Grove, Illinois

Library of Congress Cataloging-in-Publication Data

Kraft, Jim.
The no-good do-good pirates / by Jim Kraft; illustrated by Lynne Avril.
p. cm.
Summary: When Captain Squint and his band of pirates are sentenced to do a good deed,
they have problems figuring out just what is a good deed.
ISBN 978-0-8075-5695-5
[1. Pirates—Fiction. 2. Helpfulness—Fiction.] I. Avril, Lynne, 1951- ill. II. Title.
PZ7.K85845No 2008   [E]—dc22   2007052609

Printed in China through B & P International Ltd.
10 9 8 7 6 5 4 3 2 1

The design is by Carol Gildar.

For more information about Albert Whitman & Company,
please visit our web site at www.albertwhitman.com.

For Jean, Jeff, and Matt.—J.K.

To Forrest.—L.A.

Turn the page, matey!

Here's a tale of four no-good pirates—
Captain Squint, Ed the Fierce, One-Tooth Willy,
and Smelly Bob. They prowled the seas in their
ship, the *Flying Pig.*

These pirates were so bad . . .

They made teddy bears walk the plank.

They plundered children's birthday parties.

Wash behind your wig!

SOAP

They stole the governor's toy boats!

At last, these no-good pirates were caught by the law.

"Guilty!" the judge declared. "Guilty of robbing, looting, sinking, stinking, and keeping a parrot without a license!

"Luckily for you, our prison is closed for spring cleaning today," the judge continued. "So here's the deal: Do one good deed before sundown, and I'll set you free."

"What's a good deed?" Captain Squint whispered.
None of the pirates knew.

Back on the street, the pirates saw a woman filling a shop window with freshly baked pies.

"Suppose we was to eat all them pies," One-Tooth Willy suggested. "Then that lady could close the shop and snooze all afternoon. Wouldn't that be a good deed?"

"It sounds good to me!" Captain Squint declared.

The pirates barged into the shop and began stuffing pies into their mouths.

"Out! Out! You flea-bitten seadogs!" the woman screamed as she beat the pirates onto the sidewalk.

Captain Squint rubbed his sore head. "A good deed probably wouldn't feel so bad," he said. "We'd best try something else."

All day long, the pirates tried to do a good deed. At the bank, they thought it might be good to sweep the loose money into a sack. But the bank guards threw them out the door.

They thought it might be good to take candy from babies, so the candy wouldn't rot the babies' teeth. But the babies bit and the mothers bashed, until even Captain Squint hollered, "Mommy!"

Abandon candy!

Finally, the baffled and beaten pirates dragged themselves down to the harbor. "I give up," Captain Squint said. "All our good deeds have turned out bad."

"The sun's going down," Smelly Bob pointed out. "Our time is almost up."

Just then, the notorious pirate ship *Sea Monkey* sailed into the harbor.

Polly is a jailbird!

"Ahoy, Cap'n Ratbeard!" Captain Squint shouted. "Have you come to rescue us?"

"We've come to snatch every purse and piggy bank in this town!" Captain Ratbeard replied. "Men, prepare to plunder!"

His villainous crew roared nastily.

"Avast!" Captain Squint said. "And beware! This town is full of pirate-bashing ladies and bloodthirsty babies!"

Danger! Danger!

Captain Ratbeard and his men grew pale.
"Pirate-bashing ladies! Bloodthirsty
babies!" they exclaimed. "We'd better plunder
someplace safer!"
And they steered their ship back out to sea.

As the *Sea Monkey* disappeared, a cheering crowd rushed onto the dock. "Well done!" the judge said. "You did your good deed—you saved the town!"

"We did?" Captain Squint replied.

"And you beat the deadline. So you're free to leave."

"We are?" said Ed the Fierce.

When the *Flying Pig* was safely back at sea, Smelly Bob asked, "So, did we do a good deed after all?"

"Beats me," One-Tooth Willy said.

"A good deed is harder to recognize than Smelly Bob after a bath," Ed the Fierce decided.

Speak for yourself!

Captain Squint scratched his chin. "Shiver me timbers! It *is* a mystery," he declared. "But I do know one thing for sure."

"What's that?" the others asked.

"It's lucky we're good at pirating," the captain replied, "'cause at do-gooding, we're no good at all!"